The Tulip and the Comet

Based on an original drawing by Lucas Aurelio

Published by **TASHA** PUBLISHING

A division of **TASHA** PICTURES

Library of Congress:

Text copyright © 2013 by Marco Aurelio

Illustration copyright © 2013 by TASHA pictures

Original drawing copyright © by Lucas Aurelio

Printed in USA - First Edition

ISBN-10: 099111406X

ISBN-13: 978-0-9911140-6-1

Book I of The Fable Series

Dedicated to:

my mother Maria Auxiliadora

Lucas Aurelio

Isabella Rose

The Tulip and the Comet

written by

Marco Aurelio

illustrated by

Dario Vasconcellos

TASHA PUBLISHING BOOKS

It was a beautiful night

a long time ago.

A Tulip
living an uneventful life

looked up
in the sky.

She had
looked up
in the sky
before

and was well acquainted with the moon

but the moon just stood there

and there

and there.

On
this
particular
night

something
was moving up there

among the stars, past the moon, far up in the sky.

Something, she noticed, shone even brighter.

She had

never

seen

that

before.

It was

mesmerizing!

Our Tulip

had met a comet.

She caught it by chance.

She looked up

and there it was.

She looked at it until

her neck began to hurt.

She
turned
around

and looked the other way

but it was gone.

" Did you see it?"
she asked
Mrs. Tree.

But
Mrs. Tree
was
fast
asleep.

" Mr. Shrub," she thought

and turned to her neighbor
in the east.

" Did you,"

and bit her lip
in mid-sentence.

**Mr. Shrub was a cranky being

and
would not be happy
to be awoken.

Worse yet

he would complain all night.

So our Tulip
looked up again

then
to the ground

and for the first time ever

she
tried
to walk.

And
to her surprise

she

couldn't go
anywhere.

**She tried again

and again

and again.

She was
definitely
stuck.

She was desperately stuck.

She remembered a conversation awhile ago

when the Bee
came to visit.

Mr. Shrub

kept
interrupting
them.

She had suggested to Mrs. Tree that they move elsewhere.

She was no longer
happy there.

The Bee told them marvelous stories

about all the places she had been.

Taj Mahal, India

Moai Statues, Easter Island, Chile

Sugar Loaf
Rio de Janeiro, Brazil

Christ the Redeemer
Rio de Janeiro, Brazil

So our Tulip
decided at once

" That's it. I'm out of here! "

Mrs.Tree tried to convince her otherwise

and did something
she had never done

she asked Mr. Shrub to intervene.

Oh my! The stories he told.

Horrible places

chaos

fires

mayhem.

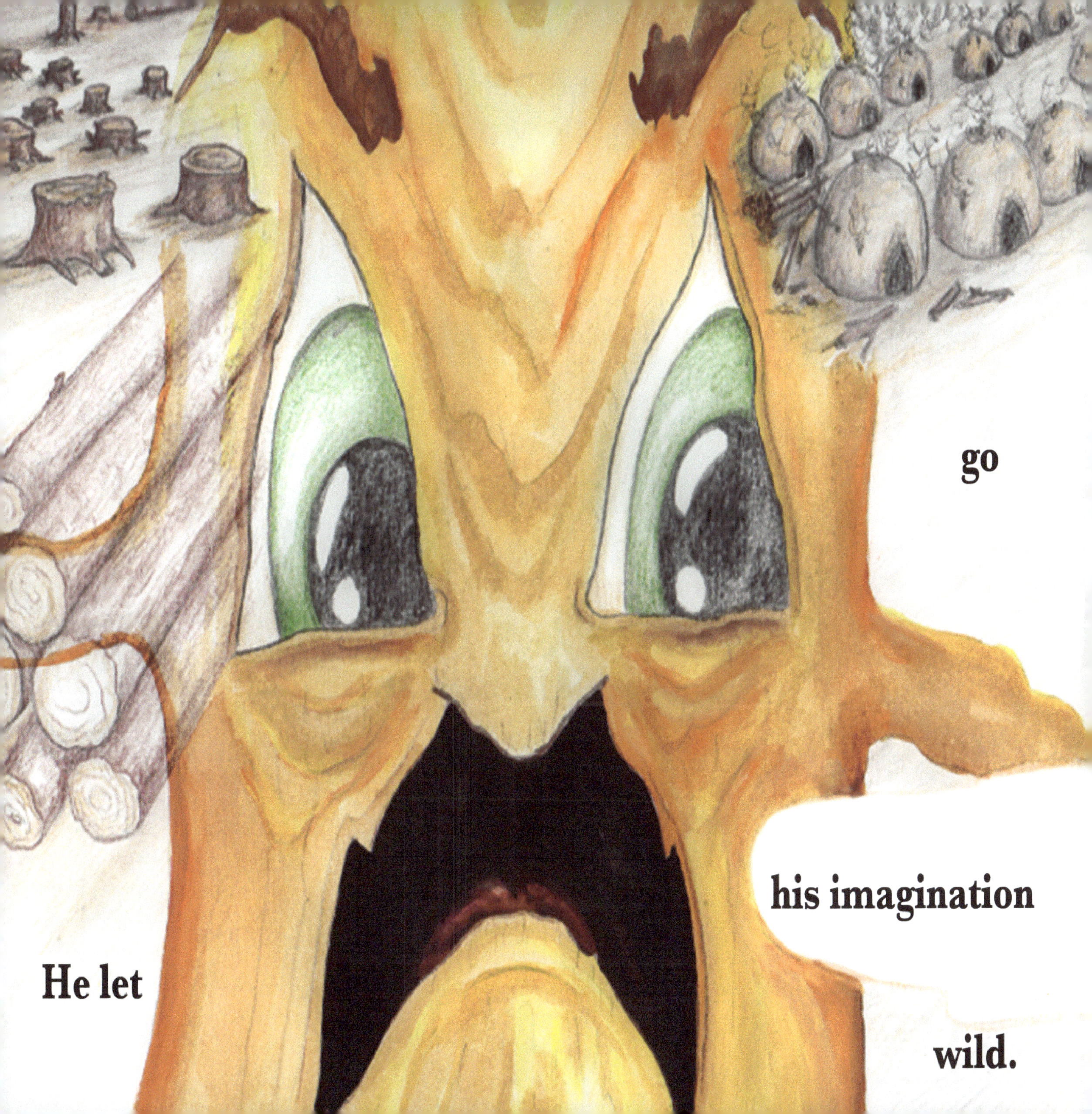
He let
go
his imagination
wild.

After he talked

and talked

and talked

our little Tulip fell asleep

and strangely enough

never thought about leaving again

until now.

But it was late

Mrs. Tree and Mr. Shrub were asleep

and it would not be polite

to leave without saying goodbye.

So she went
to sleep

dreaming of all the wonderful places

she would
one day visit.

And as she fell asleep

and asleep

one last thought
crossed her mind

" Tomorrow, I'm off to see the world."

The Next Book in The Fable Series is:

The Apple Tree on the Hill

Based on an original drawing by Lucas Aurelio